HORRiD HENRY'S
Wedding

HORRiD HENRY'S
Wedding

Francesca Simon
Illustrated by Tony Ross

Orion
Children's Books

Horrid Henry's Wedding originally appeared in
Horrid Henry Tricks the Tooth Fairy first published in Great Britain in 1997
by Orion Children's Books
This edition first published in Great Britain in 2014
by Orion Children's Books
a division of the Orion Publishing Group Ltd
Orion House
5 Upper Saint Martin's Lane
London WC2H 9EA
An Hachette UK Company

1 3 5 7 9 10 8 6 4 2

Text © Francesca Simon 1997, 2014
Illustrations © Tony Ross 2014

The right of Francesca Simon and Tony Ross to be identified
as author and illustrator of this work has been asserted.

The Orion Publishing Group's policy is to use papers that
are natural, renewable and recyclable products and made
from wood grown in sustainable forests. The logging and
manufacturing processes are expected to conform to the
environmental regulations of the country of origin.

A catalogue record for this book is available from the British Library.

ISBN 978 1 4440 0121 1
Printed in China

www.orionbooks.co.uk
www.horridhenry.co.uk

For Callum Greenfield

There are many more **Horrid Henry** books available.
For a complete list visit
www.horridhenry.co.uk
or
www.orionbooks.co.uk

Contents

Chapter 1   11

Chapter 2   21

Chapter 3   29

Chapter 4   39

Chapter 5   45

Chapter 6   55

Chapter 7   61

Chapter 1

"I'm not wearing these horrible
clothes and that's that!"
said Horrid Henry.

Horrid Henry glared at the mirror.
A stranger smothered in a lilac
ruffled shirt, green satin
knickerbockers, tights, pink
cummerbund tied in a floppy bow
and pointy white satin shoes with
gold buckles glared back at him.

Henry had never seen anyone
looking so silly in his life.

"Aha ha ha ha ha!"

shrieked Horrid Henry,
pointing at the mirror.
Then Henry peered more closely.

The ridiculous looking boy was

HIM.

Perfect Peter stood next to
Horrid Henry. He too was
smothered in a lilac ruffled shirt,
green satin knickerbockers, tights,
pink cummerbund and pointy white
shoes with gold buckles.
But unlike Henry, Peter was smiling.

"Aren't they *adorable*?"
squealed Prissy Polly.
"That's how my children are always
going to dress."

Prissy Polly was Horrid Henry's
horrible older cousin. Prissy Polly
was always squeaking and squealing:

"Eeek, it's a
speck of dust."

"Eeek, it's a puddle."

"Eeek, my hair is a mess."

But when Prissy Polly announced she was getting married to Pimply Paul and wanted Henry and Peter to be pageboys, Mum said yes before Henry could stop her.

"What's a pageboy?" asked Henry suspiciously.

"A pageboy carries the wedding rings down the aisle on a satin cushion," said Mum.

"And throws confetti afterwards," said Dad.

Henry liked the idea of throwing confetti. But carrying rings on a cushion? No thanks.

"I don't want to be a pageboy,"
said Henry.

"I do, I do,"
said Peter.

"You're going to be a pageboy,
and that's that," said Mum.

"And you'll behave yourself,"
said Dad. "It's very kind of cousin
Polly to ask you."

Henry scowled.
"Who'd want to be married to *her*?"
said Henry. "I wouldn't if you paid
me a million pounds."

But for some reason the bridegroom, Pimply Paul, did want to marry Prissy Polly. And as far as Henry knew, he had not been paid one million pounds.

Chapter 2

Pimply Paul was also trying on his wedding clothes. He looked ridiculous in a black top hat, lilac shirt, and a black jacket covered in gold swirls.

"I won't wear these silly clothes,"
said Henry.

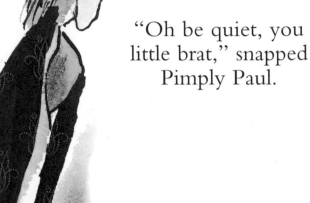

"Oh be quiet, you
little brat," snapped
Pimply Paul.

Horrid Henry
glared at him.

"I won't," said Henry.
"And that's final."

"Henry, stop being horrid,"
said Mum. She looked extremely
silly in a big floppy hat dripping
with flowers.

Suddenly Henry grabbed at the lace
ruffles round his throat.

"I'm choking," he gasped,
"I can't breathe."

Then Henry fell to the floor
and rolled around.

"*Ugggggghhhhhhh*," moaned Henry.
"I'm dying."

"Get up this minute, Henry!"
said Dad.

"Eeek, there's dirt on the floor!"
shrieked Polly.

"Can't you control that child?"
hissed Pimply Paul.

"I don't want to be a pageboy!"

howled Horrid Henry.

"Thank you so much for asking me to be a pageboy, Polly," shouted Perfect Peter, trying to be heard over Henry's screams.

"You're welcome," shouted Polly.

"Stop that, Henry!" ordered Mum.
"I've never been so ashamed in
my life."

"I hate children," muttered
Pimply Paul under his breath.

Horrid Henry stopped.
Unfortunately, his pageboy clothes
looked as fresh and crisp as ever.

All right, thought Horrid Henry.
You want me at the wedding?
You've got me.

Chapter 3

Prissy Polly's wedding day arrived.
Henry was delighted to see
rain pouring down.
How cross Polly would be.

Perfect Peter was already dressed.

"Isn't this going to be fun, Henry?"
said Peter.

"No!" said Henry, sitting on the
floor. "And I'm not going."

Mum and Dad stuffed Henry
into his pageboy clothes.
It was hard, heavy work.
Finally everyone was in the car.

"We're going
to be late!"
shrieked Mum.

"We're going
to be late!"
shrieked Dad.

"We're going to
be late!" shrieked
Perfect Peter.

"Good!" muttered Henry.

★

Mum, Dad, Henry and Peter
arrived at the church.

Boom!

There was a clap of thunder.

Rain poured down. All the other
guests were already inside.

"Watch out for the puddle, boys," said Mum, as she leapt out of the car. She opened her umbrella.

Dad jumped over the puddle.

Peter jumped over the puddle.

Henry jumped over the puddle,
and tripped.

SPLASH!

"Oopsy," said Henry.

His ruffles were torn,
his knickerbockers were filthy,
and his satin shoes were soaked.

Mum, Dad and Peter were covered
in muddy water.

Perfect Peter burst into tears.

"You've ruined my pageboy clothes,"

sobbed Peter.

Mum wiped as much dirt as she could off Henry and Peter.

"It was an accident, Mum, really,"
said Henry.

"Hurry up, you're late!"
shouted Pimply Paul.

Chapter 4

Mum and Dad dashed into the
church. Henry and Peter stayed
outside, waiting to make their
entrance.

Pimply Paul and his best man,
Cross Colin, stared at Henry
and Peter.

"You look a mess," said Paul.

"It was an accident," said Henry.

Peter snivelled.

"Now be careful with the wedding
rings," said Cross Colin.
He handed Henry and Peter
a satin cushion each, with a
gold ring on top.

A great quivering lump of lace
and taffeta and bows and flowers
approached. Henry guessed Prissy
Polly must be lurking somewhere
underneath.

"Eeek," squeaked the clump. "Why
did it have to rain on my wedding?"

"Eeek," squeaked the clump again.
"You're filthy."

Perfect Peter began to sob.
The satin cushion trembled in
his hand. The ring balanced
precariously near the edge.

Cross Colin snatched Peter's cushion.
"You can't carry a ring with your
hand shaking like that,"
snapped Colin. "You'd better
carry them both, Henry."

"Come *on*," hissed Pimply Paul.
"We're late!"

Cross Colin and Pimply Paul
dashed into the church.

Chapter 5

The music started.
Henry pranced down the aisle
after Polly.
Everyone stood up.

Henry beamed and bowed and waved. He was King Henry the Horrible, smiling graciously at his cheering subjects before he chopped off their heads.

As he danced along, he stepped
on Polly's long trailing dress.

Riiiiip.

"Eeeeek!" squeaked Prissy Polly.

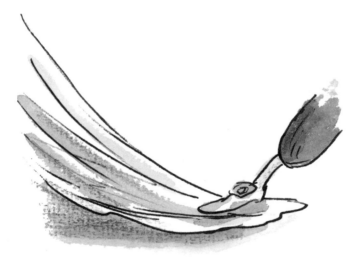

Part of Polly's train lay beneath
Henry's muddy satin shoe.
That dress was too long anyway,
thought Henry.
He picked the fabric out of the way
and stomped down the aisle.

The bride, groom, best man,
and pageboys assembled in front
of the minister.

Henry stood ...

 and stood ...

and stood.

The minister droned on … and on … and on. Henry's arm holding up the cushion began to ache.

This is boring, thought Henry, jiggling the rings on the cushion.

Boing! Boing! Boing!

Oooh, thought Henry.
I'm good at ring tossing.

The rings bounced.

The minister droned.

Henry was a famous pancake chef,
tossing the pancakes higher and
higher and higher…

Clink clunk.

The rings rolled down the aisle and
vanished down a small grate.

Oops, thought Henry.

"May I have the rings, please?"
said the minister.

Everyone looked at Henry.

"He's got them," said Henry
desperately, pointing at Peter.

"I have not," sobbed Peter.

Henry reached into his pocket.
He found two pieces of old
chewing-gum, some gravel,
and his lucky pirate ring.

"Here, use this," he said.

Chapter 6

At last, Pimply Paul and Prissy Polly were married.

Cross Colin handed Henry and Peter a basket of pink and yellow rose petals each.

"Throw the petals in front of the
bride and groom as they walk back
down the aisle," whispered Colin.

"I will," said Peter.
He scattered the petals before
Pimply Paul and Prissy Polly.

"So will I," said Henry.
He hurled a handful of petals
in Pimply Paul's face.

"Watch it, you little brat,"
snarled Paul.

"Windy, isn't it?" said Henry.
He hurled another handful of petals
at Polly.

"Eeek," squeaked Prissy Polly.

"Everyone outside for photographs,"
said the photographer.
Horrid Henry loved having his
picture taken. He dashed out.
"Pictures of the bride and groom
first," said the photographer.

Henry jumped in front.

Click.

Henry peeked from the side.

Click.

Henry stuck out his tongue.

Click.

Henry made horrible rude faces.

Click.

"This way to the reception!"
said Cross Colin.

Chapter 7

The wedding party was held
in a nearby hotel.

The adults did nothing but talk and
eat, talk and drink, talk and eat.

Perfect Peter sat at the table
and ate his lunch.

Horrid Henry sat under the table
and poked people's legs. He crawled
around and squashed some toes.
Then Henry got bored and drifted
into the next room.

There was the wedding cake,
standing alone, on a table. It was the
most beautiful, delicious-looking
cake Henry had ever seen. It had
three layers and was covered in
luscious white icing and yummy iced
flowers and bells and leaves.

Henry's mouth watered.
I'll just taste a teeny weeny bit
of petal, thought Henry.
No harm in that.

He broke off a morsel and popped
it in his mouth.

Hmmmmm boy!

That icing tasted great.

Perhaps just one more bite,
thought Henry. If I take it from
the back, no one will notice.

Henry carefully selected an icing rose
from the bottom tier and stuffed it
in his mouth.

Wow.

Henry stood back from the cake.
It looked a little uneven now, with
that rose missing from the bottom.

I'll just even it up, thought Henry.
It was the work of a moment to
break off a rose from the middle tier
and another from the top.

Then a strange thing happened.

"Eat me,"

whispered the cake.

"Go on."

Who was Henry to ignore such
a request?

He picked out a few crumbs
from the back.
Delicious, thought Henry.
Then he took a few more.
And a few more.
Then he dug out a nice big chunk.

"What do you think you're doing?"
shouted Pimply Paul.

Henry ran round the cake table.
Paul ran after him.
Round and round and round
the cake they ran.

"Just wait till I get my hands
on you!" snarled Pimply Paul.

Henry dashed under the table.
Pimply Paul lunged for him
and missed.

SPLAT!

Pimply Paul fell head first
on to the cake.

Henry slipped away.

Prissy Polly ran into the room.

"Eeek,"
she shrieked.

"Wasn't that a lovely wedding,"
sighed Mum on the way home.
"Funny they didn't have a cake,
though."

"Oh yes," said Dad.

"Oh yes," said Peter.

"Oh yes!" said Henry.
"I'll be glad to be a pageboy
anytime."

What are you going to read next?

Have more adventures with Horrid Henry,

and travel the world with

Miranda the Explorer.

Play clever tricks with Twit,

spend Mondays at Monster School,

and even brave The Dragon's Dentist . . .

Learn how love is just like a Woolly Hat,

dance under The Little Nut Tree,

take home Monstar, the best pet ever,

and have an extra-special Mr Monkey birthday party!

Enjoy all the Early Readers.

Collect all the
Horrid Henry storybooks!

Horrid Henry

Horrid Henry
and the Secret Club

Horrid Henry Tricks
the Tooth Fairy

Horrid Henry
Gets Rich Quick

Horrid Henry's Nits

Horrid Henry's
Haunted House

Horrid Henry and
the Mummy's Curse

Horrid Henry's
Revenge

Horrid Henry and the
Bogey Babysitter

Horrid Henry's Stinkbomb

Horrid Henry's
Underpants

Horrid Henry
Meets the Queen

Horrid Henry and
the Mega Mean
Time Machine

Horrid Henry and
the Football Fiend

Horrid Henry's
Christmas Cracker

Horrid Henry and
the Abominable
Snowman

Horrid Henry Robs the Bank

Horrid Henry
Wakes the Dead

Horrid Henry Rocks

Horrid Henry and
the Zombie Vampire

Horrid Henry's Monster Movie

the orion star